TRAINS

Steaming! *Pulling!* Huffing!

by Patricia Hubbell

illustrated by Megan Halsey and Sean Addy

two lions

For Wanda
—P. H.

For the R3 and my NYC
trains, #642 and #172
—M. H.

To my sons
Aidan and Elijah.
And to Tyler, Kendra, and
Jordan. You guys rock!
—S. A.

two lions

Amazon Publishing, Attn: Amazon Children's Publishing,
P.O. Box 400818, Las Vegas, NV 89140
www.amazon.com/amazonchildrenspublishing

Library of Congress Cataloging-in-Publication Data

Hubbell, Patricia.
Trains : steaming! pulling! huffing! / by Patricia Hubbell ;
illustrated by Megan Halsey and Sean Addy. — 1st ed.
p. cm.
Summary: Rhyming text presents the characteristics of various
kinds of trains.
ISBN 978-0-7614-5593-6
[1. Railroads—Trains—Fiction. 2. Stories in rhyme.]
I. Halsey, Megan, ill. II. Addy, Sean, ill. III. Title.

PZ8.3.H848Tr 2005
[E]—dc22

2004014468

The text of this book is
set in Geometric 415.
The illustrations are rendered
in clip art, etchings,
original drawings, and maps.

Book design by
Adam Mietlowski
Printed in China

Robo-Rail

Trains! Trains! Trains!
Silver trains. Black trains.
Speeding-down-the-track trains.

Passenger trains.

Freight trains.

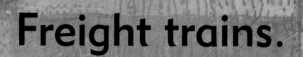

Crossing-every-state trains.

Electric trains.   Diesel trains.

Big old smoky steam trains.

Zoo trains.

Subway trains.

Taking-me-to-you trains.

Freights that rumble, rock, and ROAR.

Boxcars rolling
more . . .
and MORE!

Smokestack. Tender. Coupling. Gear.

Red caboose brings up the rear.

Race through valleys.
Climb up ridges.
Whoosh through tunnels.
Cross high bridges.

Giant engines snorting, puffing.

Steaming! Pulling! Rushing! Huffing!

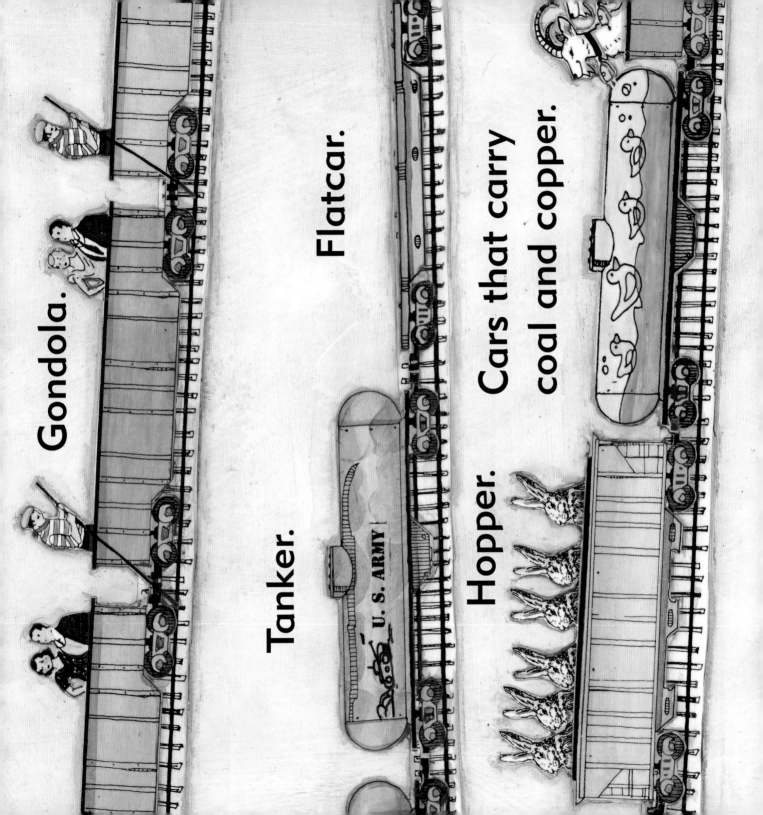

Gondola.

Flatcar.

Tanker.

Hopper.

Cars that carry
coal and copper.

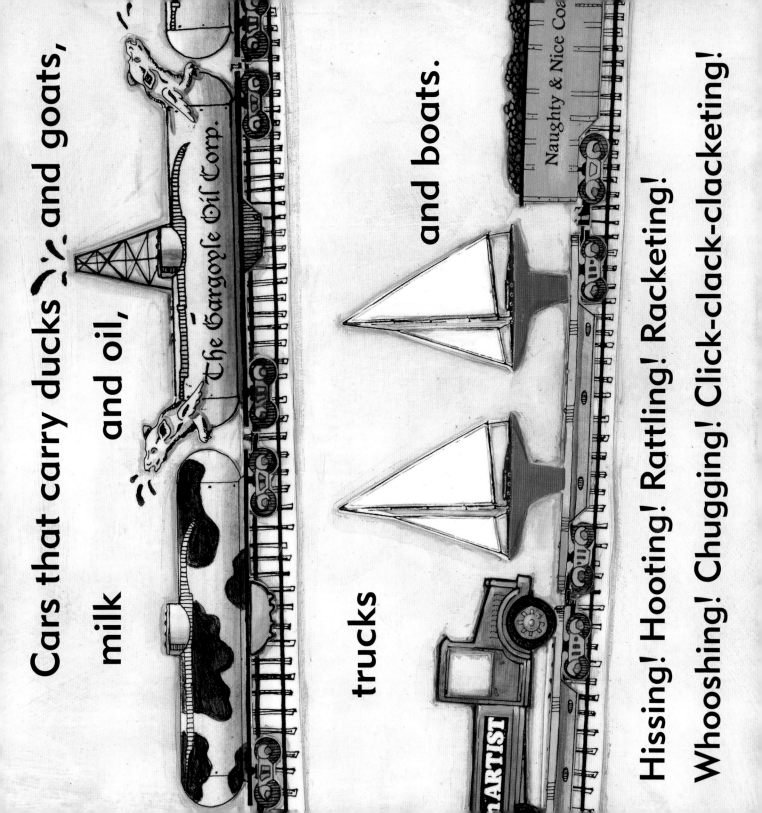

Cars that carry ducks and goats,

milk and oil,

trucks and boats.

Hissing! Hooting! Rattling! Racketing!
Whooshing! Chugging! Click-clack-clacketing!

Zoooom! Zoooom! Fast streamliner!
Sleeper. Club car. Coach car. Diner.

Coach Car

Sleek strong engine, sparkling new!
Dome car's where you see the view.

Conductor. Porter. Engineer.

Cook

Porter

Engineer

Cook and waiter.
Lunchtime's here!

Conductor

Waiter

Greetings from the USA

Have a sandwich. Have a snack.
Silver Zephyr's on the track.

Taking folks on their vacation.

All across our great **big** nation.

Trains go dashing through the night.

Tracks lit up by beaming light.

Trains that stop and go and jerk,
take my mom and dad to work.

School
Bus Stop

Clickety-clickety-
clickety-clack!
Commuter train
will bring them back.

Toy train,
block train,
pulls me fast.

Tooting, hooting,
home at last!

North
and South
and East
and West.

I think we are lost.

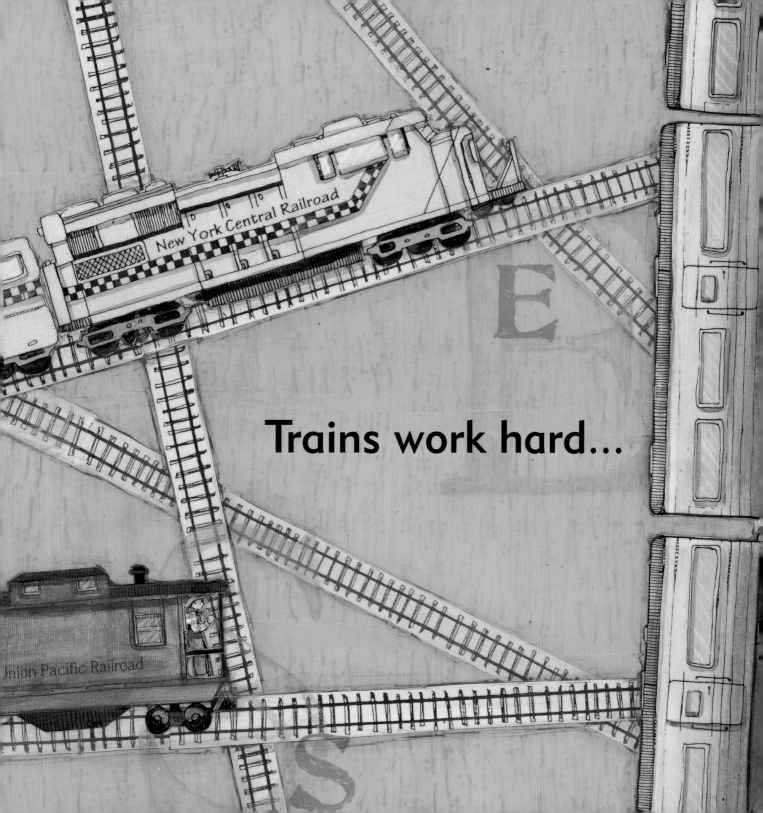

Trains work hard...

...and then they rest.